IF I COULD DRIVE A
CRANE!

by Michael Teitelbaum
Illustrated by Uldis Klavins

SCHOLASTIC INC.
New York   Toronto   London   Auckland   Sydney
Mexico City   New Delhi   Hong Kong   Buenos Aires

TONKA™ is a trademark of Hasbro, Inc.
Used with permission.
Copyright © 2002 Hasbro, Inc.
All rights reserved. Published by Scholastic Inc.
SCHOLASTIC and associated logos are trademarks and/or registered trademarks of Scholastic Inc.

Library of Congress Cataloging-in-Publication Data

Teitelbaum, Michael.
    If I could drive a crane! / by Michael Teitelbaum; illustrated by Uldis Klavins
        p. cm.
Summary: A young boy imagines all the things he could do if he operated a crane.
ISBN 0-439-34174-4 (pbk.)
    [1. Cranes, derricks, etc. -- Fiction.] I. Klavins, Uldis, ill. II. Title.

PZ7.T233 If 2002
[E]--dc21   2001042023

ISBN 0-439-34174-4

10 9 8 7 6 5 4 3   03 04 05 06

Printed in the U.S.A.
First Scholastic printing, May 2002

My name is Tyler. I think that playing with trucks is the best! My favorite truck is the crane.

I would move heavy loads from one place to another. That's what cranes are for.

There are lots of different kinds of cranes, and I would drive them all!

A truck crane has wheels and can go anywhere a regular truck can go. I drive it on the highway to get to a construction site.

Before I can use my truck crane, I have to put down special legs called outriggers. These strong metal legs help keep the crane steady when I'm lifting big loads.

Now my truck crane is ready to work. I can extend the crane's arm to make it bigger. I can also rotate the crane to move a load from one place to another.

When I attach a big bucket to the end of the crane's main cable, I can use the crane to dig and to move gravel.

A truck has brought huge bundles of lumber to the construction site. I attach grappling tines to the end of the crane's cable. Now my truck crane can unload the lumber. Then I can move it to exactly where it's needed.

By attaching a large magnet to the end of the cable, my truck crane can lift heavy pieces of steel.

Construction beams and girders are the first parts used when a new building is started. With its magnet, the crane can move the parts with no problem.

Another kind of crane is the crawler crane. It doesn't have wheels like a truck crane.

Instead, a crawler crane moves on special treads, just like a bulldozer. These treads help the crawler crane work in soft, muddy areas.

I'm using my crawler crane to help remove fallen trees from this flooded area.

For the biggest and heaviest loads of all, I use a bridge crane. It's also called a gantry crane.

A bridge crane's legs are very tall and far apart.

I use my bridge crane at a seaport. There I unload big, heavy crates from arriving ships. I lift the crates out of the ships, then place them onto flatbed trucks that drive them away.

My bridge crane can swivel to move its load.

It can also move its load by rolling along on tracks, just like a train. But a bridge crane moves slowly, and trains move really fast!

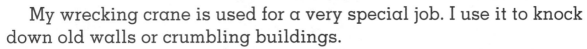

My wrecking crane is used for a very special job. I use it to knock down old walls or crumbling buildings.

A big, heavy wrecking ball hangs from the crane's main cable. Another cable, which I control, pulls the wrecking ball back. When I let the ball go, it swings into the wall and knocks it down.

I'd use all kinds of cranes, for all kinds of jobs, if I could drive a crane!